THERE WAS ONCE A GROUP OF TREES
who were fed up with living in a deep,
dark and crowded valley. So they decided
to move to the brow of a nearby hill.

Here, they could enjoy the sun on their
leaves, fresh air through their branches
and the best view for miles around.

But trees cannot walk without magic.
And the creatures that followed them created
an enchanted forest. Outside, *darker*
creatures wanted the magic for themselves.

This is the story of how a little boy came
into the forest, and left the way open...

For Gina, Mark, Matthew and Nicholas
Thank you to Anne McNeil and David Mackintosh

Love to Monika

THE TALE OF JACK FROST
by David Melling

British Library Cataloguing in Publication Data
A catalogue record of this book is available from
the British Library.

ISBN 0 340 85200 3 (PB)

ISBN 0 340 85199 6 (HB)

Copyright © David Melling 2003

The right of David Melling to be identified
as the author and illustrator of this Work has
been asserted by him in accordance with
the Copyright, Designs and Patents Act 1988.

First HB edition published 2003
This PB edition published 2004

10 9 8 7 6 5 4 3 2 1

Published by Hodder Children's Books
a division of Hodder Headline Limited
338 Euston Road London NW1 3BH

Printed in China

THE TALE OF
JACK FROST

DAVID MELLING

Hodder Children's Books

A division of Hodder Headline Limited

It was a crisp and frosty morning.
Woodwind and Woffle were out collecting
snow-beetles when they found a boy.

A *real* boy, asleep in the snow.

They hopped around in circles.
'What to do! What to do!' they squeaked.

Shadows came bobbing and gliding towards them from every direction.

Unicorns and woodhoppers and beezels appeared.
Owls and magpies and skitlets dropped from bending
branches. Funny looking creatures peered around each
other, and even the trees shuffled forward for a better look.

Cowslip, a tall and gentle creature
with hairy knees, spoke first.
'What shall we do with him?'
he asked.

The unicorn stepped forward.

'We are in danger,' he said.
'Where he came in, others will
follow.'

But Woodwind and Woffle were
hopping again.
'Too cold! Too cold!' they cried.
'He needs our help.'
Cowslip agreed. He prepared an
ointment and bathed the boy's eyes.

Slowly, the boy awoke.

They asked him many questions,
but he remembered nothing.
Not even his name.

They all taught the boy
what they knew.

He mixed rare potions and
unusual soups — his favourite
was worm-juice surprise.

He was quick to understand magic,
and he was *very* good with snail glue.

But his skin was snow white and always ice cold.
Whatever he touched for more than a few
moments turned to frost.

And so the creatures named him Jack Frost.
Only the unicorn remained nervous.
'Something bad will happen,' he snorted.

And before long, it did...

Now, in the dank valley with its curling mist there lived many thick stubby creatures with green oily skin.

Goblins!!

They smelled of boiled cabbage and liked to make rude noises just for fun. Clever, they were not. When they heard that Jack Frost, a *real* boy, had been shown the magic of the enchanted forest they were furious. Goblins believed that the magic should be theirs.

Now the forest was open – this was their chance.

That night, Jack Frost was playing with a friendly pack of Bing Bong Bandylegs. These were large animals, but they scared easily. Indeed, at the first sign of danger they would roll on to their backs and pretend to be asleep.

So when a goblin stumbled across Jack Frost, with a bunch of snoring creatures, he stuffed him into a sack and scurried off, back to the goblins' lair.

King Gobbledegook plucked Jack from the sack.
He was surrounded by cabbage-smelling goblins.
'Hello,' said Jack, bravely, and touched the royal
dimply nose.

'Eeeeeaaarrrgghh!' squealed the king,
'he's freezing!'

'WE WANT THE MAGIC!!' roared the goblins.

'I'LL do the shouting,' snapped King Gobbledegook.
He turned to Jack. 'YOU'RE going to tell us how to
get this magic,' he said, 'or there'll be trouble.
And YOU'LL be in it.'

The other goblins sniggered.

'That's easy!' said Jack. 'Every
night the sun goes to sleep in
a lake by the forest. It is full of
magic and easy to catch.'

'Ooooooo!' said the goblins.
They were impressed.

'But if I show you how to catch
the sun you must promise never
to go into the enchanted forest,'
said Jack.

'Oh yes,' they said, giggling and nudging
each other in the ribs, 'we promise.'

Jack knew they were lying, but he had an idea.

The goblins followed Jack to the lake. They were very excited.
'First, you must make a circle around the lake,' said Jack. 'Now look
into the lake and tell me what you see.'

The goblins stared. Nothing. Then a small goblin, who had medals for
thinking, sprang to his feet. 'Water!' he shouted.

'No!' said Jack, and pointed at the reflection of the moon. 'Look, *there* is the sun.' He dipped his finger into the lake. With wide eyes the goblins gawped as a thin film of frost crept and crackled and glistened across the lake.

In moments it had turned to ice.

Well, the goblins were delighted. They lifted the 'frozen sun' and ran off.
They didn't even say thank you.

But, by the time they reached the stone tower, the ice had melted and the sun had gone. All they had were wet hands.

'We've been tricked,' growled King Gobbledegook.

With screams of rage, they raced back to Jack.

Jack had been making magic ice puddles with snail glue,
when he heard angry slippy noises:

SQUEEE-DUNK!!!

As soon as the goblins touched the ice puddles they froze.
Within moments there were frozen goblins everywhere.

Jack skipped to the ice statues and gave them a frosty
sunflower. 'Here you are,' he laughed. 'This is your sun.
These sunflowers will warm you up and set you free.
This is the only magic you will see tonight!'

The goblins could only stare with stiff grins and
chattering teeth.

Woodwind and Woffle rushed to meet Jack.

'No more goblins! No more goblins!' they sang.

'We must celebrate at once,' said the unicorn, who
could see how brave Jack had been.
Everyone cheered with delight.

All night there was music, magic,
and worm-juice surprise.

Jack was so happy he tingled all over. He could feel himself
getting lighter and lighter. Then he was flying.

Jack never did remember his past, but, at last, he knew where he belonged. And the goblins? Well, they're still looking for the magic, and they're still grumpy. But that's goblins for you.

Sometimes on cold winter nights you may see
swirling shapes of ice on your windows,
or frosty ice puddles in your garden.

Yes! Jack Frost likes to visit places outside the enchanted forest
and he always leaves little spells of magic –
to protect you from the smell of boiled cabbage.